The Night Before KIDS' YOGA DAY

by TERESA ANNE POWER

illustrated by ANNA ABRAMSKAYA

STAFFORD HOUSE BOOKS

"This book is dedicated to all the amazing Kids' Yoga Day Ambassadors who took the challenge to inspire children to practice yoga on Kids' Yoga Day and beyond."
—T.P.

The Night Before Kids' Yoga Day
Copyright © 2020 by Teresa Anne Power

All rights reserved. No part of this book may be used or reproduced in any manner whatsoever without written permission except in the case of brief quotations embodied in critical articles and reviews.

For information address:
Stafford House Books, Inc.
P.O. Box 291, Pacific Palisades, CA 90272
www.staffordhousebooks.com

The author and publisher disclaim any liability in connection with the exercises and advice contained herein.

Library of Congress Control Number: 2020934221
ISBN: 978-1-7344786-2-4 Hardback
ISBN: 978-1-7344786-3-1 E-Book

printed in China

A read-aloud poem by Teresa Anne Power, Kids' Yoga Day creator and bestselling author of the *ABCs of Yoga for Kids* and *Little Mouse Adventures* series.

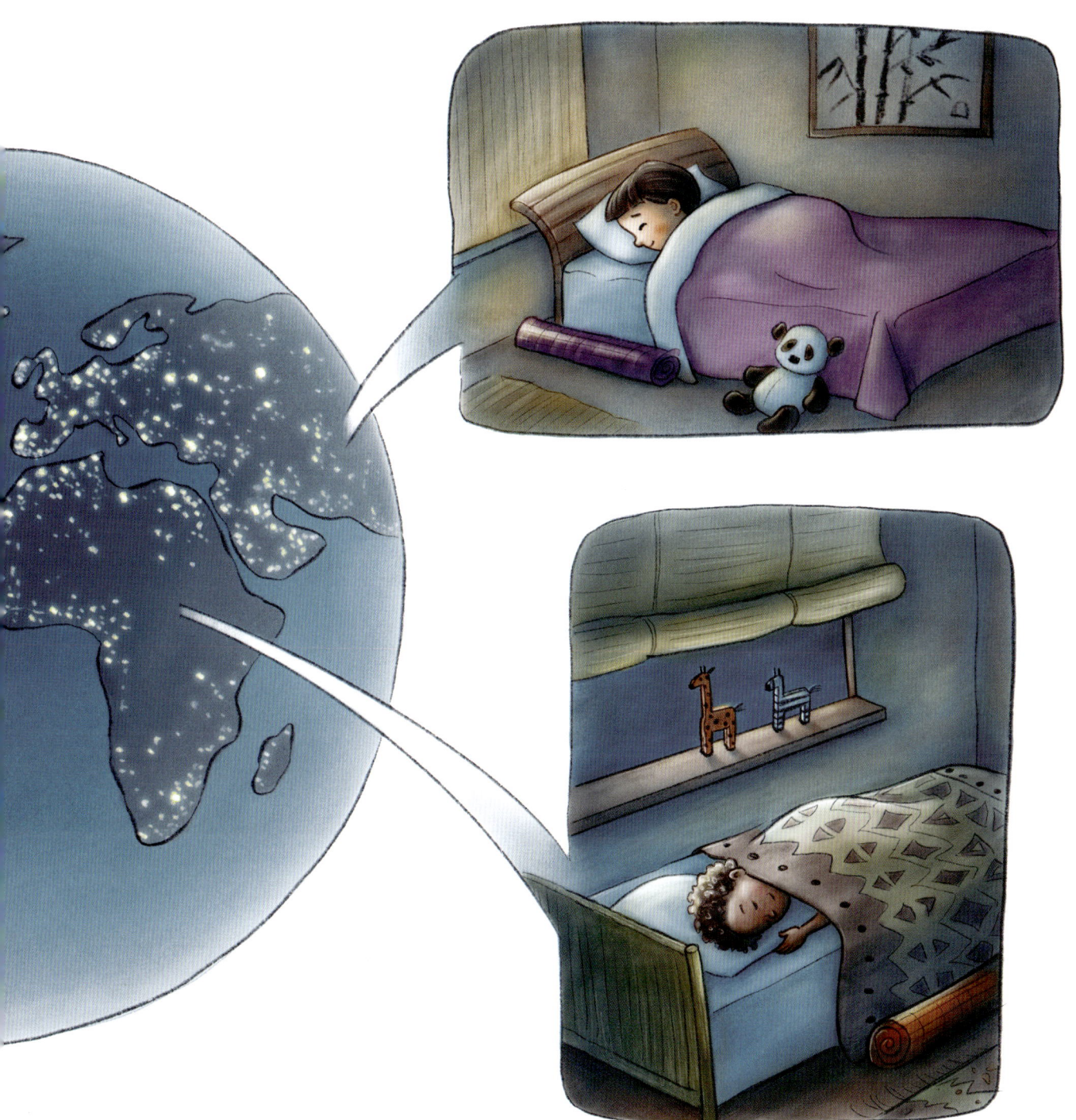

'Twas the night before Kids' Yoga Day, when all around the world,
not a soul was stirring, no one moved or uncurled.
Yoga mats had been placed by each child's bed with care,
the anticipation of Kids' Yoga Day filling the air.

The children were drifting off into a sound sleep,
by counting yoga poses instead of sheep.
And father in his robe and I, in my yoga pants of red,
were just heading upstairs to climb into bed.

When out in the yard I heard such a strange sound, that I peered outside and looked all around.

The moon shone so bright,
on this cloudless spring night,
that it amazed me to see
a group of children stretching on their hands and their knees!

I couldn't believe my eyes,
as I saw them practice unicorn pose beneath nighttime skies.
I watched in awe as the scene continued to unfold,
the children quietly doing yoga, without being told.

The neighborhood came alive
as other kids started to arrive.
The leader was a young girl
with a head full of curls,
Who commanded the attention
of all the boys and girls.

She then stood tall in queen pose, so regal and proud,
inviting everyone to give it a try in the crowd.
As they followed her every move,
the group got into a yoga groove.

Beneath the stars so bright,
the children stretched their bodies into the shape of a kite.

I was enamored with the little girl's poise,
as she bent her body backwards, never making a noise.
She calmly stretched her arms behind her in waterfall pose,
her cheeks glowing pink like a beautiful rose.

Next, she folded forward like a rag doll,
allowing her head and arms down to fall.
I then bent forward to touch my own toes,
while calmly breathing in and out through my nose.

Excited to see what pose was about to take place,
I peeked out of the window with a smile on my face.
The children were taking on the form of a twirling windmill,
relaxing in unison, spread out on the hill.

They stood with their legs slightly bent, with feet wide apart,
each bringing a hand to the ground in line with their heart.
I watched as they sent their other arm up toward the sky,
extending it long and reaching up high.

As they made their bodies stretch like a letter Y,
I realized why yoga is so important to try.
The children were finding a sense of calm and of peace,
which, after each yoga pose, only seemed to increase.

Soon, they were at it again,
switching poses while finding their zen.
This time they took on the shape of a chair,
by bending their knees and bringing their hands up in the air.

While letting out a contented sigh,
I sunk low, stretching my arms to the sky.
Then the little girl winked at me,
looking peaceful and stress-free.

Signaling that there were only three poses to go,
the young yogi imitated the stance of a flamingo.
Standing tall and holding her knee,
she balanced on one foot, as stable as can be.

I marveled at the concentration needed for each standing pose,
which was made easier by breathing in and out through one's nose.
The children continued to follow along,
shifting into tree pose, staying focused and strong.

Easy pose ended the yoga routine,
and I marveled again at the wondrous scene.
All the kids were now sitting with legs crossed and backs straight,
eyes closed, breathing deeply and counting slowly to eight.

Then the little girl happily sprang to her feet,
and back to their homes did the children retreat.
But I heard her exclaim as she was walking away . . .

and to all a good day!

Unicorn

Queen

Kite

Waterfall

Easy Pose

Tree

Flamingo

Rag Doll

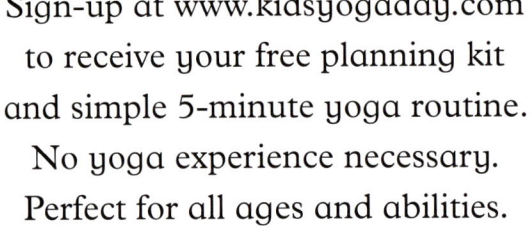

The Night Before
KIDS' YOGA DAY

was written in honor of annual Kids' Yoga Day, which is celebrated globally on the first Friday in April every year by tens of thousands of children and their teachers, parents, educators, and caregivers.

Sign-up at www.kidsyogaday.com to receive your free planning kit and simple 5-minute yoga routine. No yoga experience necessary. Perfect for all ages and abilities.

Windmill

Dog

Chair

Y

Rocking Horse

Cobra